KT-529-081

For Sylvia Kyle, Ruth Ann Johnson,
Rebecca Lim and Tad Beagley

The Mitten

A Ukrainian Folktale
adapted and illustrated by

JAN BRETT

MACDONALD YOUNG BOOKS

FALKIRK COUNCIL

FOR SCHOOLS

With special thanks to my
Ukrainian friend, Oksana Piaseckyj

First published in Great Britain in 1990 by Simon & Schuster Young Books

First published in paperback in 1999 by Macdonald Young Books
61 Western Road, Hove
East Sussex, BN3 1JD

Text and illustrations copyright © Jan Brett

All rights reserved
This book, or parts of, may not be reproduced in any form without permission
in writing from the Publishers.

Original American edition published in the US in 1989
by G. P. Putnam's Sons, New York.

Airbrush backgrounds by Joseph Hearne
Typeset by Goodfellow & Egon
Phototypesetting Limited, Cambridge

Printed and bound in Belgium by Proost International Book Production

British Library Cataloguing in Publication Data

ISBN: 0 7500 2867 X

Once there was a boy named Nicki who wanted his new
mittens made from wool as white as snow.

At first, his grandmother, Baba, did not want to knit white mittens.

"If you drop one in the snow," she warned, "you'll never find it."

But Nicki wanted snow-white mittens, and finally Baba
made them.

After she finished she said, "When you come home, first I will look to see if you are safe and sound, but then I will look to see if you still have your snow-white mittens."

So off Nicki went. And it wasn't long until one of his new mittens dropped in the snow and was left behind.

A mole, tired from tunnelling along, discovered the mitten and burrowed inside. It was cozy and warm and just the right size, so he decided to stay.

A snowy-white rabbit came hopping by. He stopped for a
moment to admire his winter coat. It was then that he saw
the mitten, and he wiggled in, feet first. The mole didn't
think there was room for both of them, but when he saw
the rabbit's big hind feet he moved over.

Next a hedgehog came snuffling along. Having spent the
day looking under wet leaves for things to eat, he decided to
move into the mitten and warm himself. The mole and the
rabbit were bumped and jostled, but not being ones to argue
with someone covered with prickles, they made room.

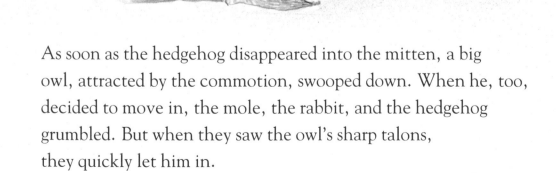

As soon as the hedgehog disappeared into the mitten, a big
owl, attracted by the commotion, swooped down. When he, too,
decided to move in, the mole, the rabbit, and the hedgehog
grumbled. But when they saw the owl's sharp talons,
they quickly let him in.

Up through the snow appeared a badger. He eyed the mitten
and began to climb in. The mole, the rabbit, the hedgehog,
and the owl were not pleased. There was no room left,
but when they saw his claws, they made some space.

It started snowing, but the animals were snug in the mitten. A waft of warm steam rose in the air, and a fox trotting by stopped to investigate. Just the sight of the cozy mitten made him feel drowsy. The fox poked his muzzle in. When the mole, the rabbit, the hedgehog, the owl, and the badger saw his shiny teeth, they gave the fox lots of room.

A great bear lumbered by. He spied the mitten all plumped up. Not being one to be left out in the cold, he began to nose his way in. The animals were packed in as tightly as could be. But what animal would argue with a bear?

The mitten swelled and stretched. It was pulled and bulged
to many times it size. But Baba's good knitting held fast.

Along came a meadow mouse, no bigger than an acorn. She wriggled into the one space left, and made herself comfortable on top of the great bear's nose.

The bear, tickled by the mouse's whiskers, gave an
enormous sneeze.
Aaaaa-aaaaa-aaaaa-ca-chew!
The force of the sneeze shot the mitten up into the sky,
and scattered the animals in all directions.

On his way home, Nicki saw a white shape in the distance.
It was the lost mitten silhouetted against the blue sky.

As he ran to catch his snow-white mitten, he saw Baba's
face in the window. First she looked to see if he was safe and
sound, and then she saw that he still had his new mittens.

FALKIRK
LIBRARY SUPPORT
FOR SCHOOLS